The Never-Ending Adventures of Cloud and Penelope

Books 1, 2 & 3

Jill A. Logan

For Savannah and Riley

Thank you for your never-ending curiosity.

Book 1

Calypso Returns

Chapter 1

It was a beautiful morning for a run through Paradise Valley. The dew made the wildflowers glisten like thousands of colorful gems in the tall, wavy grass of the vast meadow. Cloud shook her long, white mane, reared up and sprang into the air, hitting the ground at a full gallop.

Today was a very special day. Cloud was turning five. This was the day she would begin learning the secret recipes her father, Plato, had painstakingly created throughout the decades - the magical recipes for all the potions and elixirs that kept the unicorns healthy.

As she ran, Cloud pictured her father's shop, crowded with row after row of curved chunks of pine bark, all full of leaves and flowers - each with a special function.

It would be a challenge to learn everything her father knew, but she had been paying close attention to the many herbs since she was a tiny filly.

In a way, Cloud had always been prepared for this day. You see, she was born with a wondrous gift – she knew all the plants in her world by sight, smell and taste. It was instinctive, just like her father's ability to do the same.

As soon as she learned all the complicated recipes and finished her apprenticeship, she would become the herd's healer, a role her father had filled and excelled at for decades.

But all was not as straightforward as it appeared. Cloud's older sister, Penelope, had other ideas for this special day. Penelope believed the job of herd doctor belonged to her. She was the eldest, after all.

Unfortunately, Penelope wasn't born with the gift of plant-recognition; instead, she was born with the overwhelming desire for power and control. She had grown quite adept at covering this urge up. She could smile sympathetically and look concerned around sick herd members, but deep down, she despised weakness in any form. She secretly believed if a herd member got sick, they should be thrown out of Paradise Valley.

While Cloud was frolicking through the lush meadow, Penelope was putting a diabolical plan into effect. She, too, knew the importance of this day, not just for Cloud's future, but for her own.

Before this day was through, Penelope would see that their father fell ill and that she would be the only one able to cure him.

Her plan was flawless, so she thought. She had switched her father's daily breakfast of grains and healthy herbs with one of grains and a poisonous herb. Only she knew the added herb and her father would conveniently eat any evidence. Then she would miraculously cure him, as Cloud stood helplessly by.

Cloud would lose all credibility, and the herd would gather around their hero, Penelope. She'd be a shoo-in for herd doctor.

Just as Cloud reached the farthest end of the meadow, Penelope "thoughtfully" brought her father his fateful breakfast.

Plato was pleasantly surprised by her gesture. He had been worried that she'd be envious of Cloud on this special day. He ate the entire concoction at Penelope's insistence.

Soon after, he felt strange, but wrote it off to excitement – the big event would start soon. There would be food aplenty and prancing until dark.

But Plato should not have underestimated Penelope's capacity for envy and malevolence.

As the time for the ceremony drew near, the herd gathered around Plato's shop. The excitement and joy were contagious. Piles of delicious grasses and herbs filled the courtyard. The rhythm-keepers drummed out a beat with their hooves. All was in place for Cloud's big day.

As Plato and Cloud entered the courtyard, the crowd became silent. Plato slowly climbed atop the speaking mound and looked out over the huge gathering. Just as he started his speech, he felt a sudden sharp pain in his belly. He tried to ignore it, but it got worse. He tried to talk, but his voice was too weak to be heard. He slowly dropped to his knees and put his muzzle on the ground for support.

Cloud and Penelope ran to his side.

"Father, what is it?" Cloud cried.

Plato could only shake his head slowly, too weak to speak.

Penelope pretended to closely inspect her father and quickly announced that she knew what was wrong with him. She ran into his shop and reemerged with a bark carrier containing a bright green herb.

"Eat this, Father!"

Plato slowly chewed the herb, but instead of getting better, his condition kept worsening. He was now groaning with pain.

Cloud looked closely at this green herb and recognized it as anise hyssop leaf, a powerful calming agent, but capable of little else. She asked Penelope why she'd brought that to their father.

Penelope stammered an incoherent answer. She had a look of panic on her face as she told Plato to eat more. But as he swallowed another mouthful, it was very apparent the anise wasn't working as she expected.

Unsure what to do and seeing her father failing rapidly, she pulled Cloud aside and confessed to putting a dangerous herb in his breakfast. Cloud calmly asked what this herb was and upon hearing the answer, knew exactly what she had to do.

That herb was no ordinary herb. It was of the cassava strain. Not a strain to be trifled with and definitely not one that anise hyssop could cure.

Cloud ran into Plato's shop and pushed her head through the vine handle of an empty bark carrier. She spun on her heels and galloped toward Crystal Peak. As she passed through the huge crowd, she instructed them to keep Plato safe and warm.

Time was of the essence, and she hoped Mother Nature would smile kindly on her so she would not find that the delicate plant that contained the only remedy to cassava poisoning was frozen.

Cloud raced across the meadow, then followed Avalanche Creek as it snaked through the thick forest at the base of Crystal Peak.

The trail along the creek was steep and rocky as it wove its way through the huge pines, but Cloud didn't dare slow down. Time was not on her father's side. She stumbled and slipped repeatedly, but sheer will kept her on her feet.

She rounded a sharp bend in the trail and slid to a stop. Before her was a massive boulder field. The trail had been completely blocked by a rockslide.

As Cloud contemplated her dilemma, down below in Paradise Valley, Penelope quietly snuck away from the worried herd and galloped toward the edge of the valley. She knew the way all too well, for she'd taken this path many times over the past weeks. This was the path to a neighboring herd's territory.

She had been secretly meeting with their leader, Brutus. He had promised her the fame and notoriety that would come from saving her father's life and becoming her herd's doctor. He had even gathered the cassava root for her.

As she approached his herd, she instantly picked him out, for he towered above the rest. He left the herd and slowly walked toward her.

"Well? Are you loved by all?" he snickered arrogantly.

"It didn't work! My father is gravely ill. You promised me he'd be fine! What went wrong?"

"Foolish, selfish girl, did you really think I'd pass up the opportunity to 'retire' one of my 'beloved' arch rivals? With Plato unable to work, I'd be invited into your herd to lend my support. They'd need my leadership and medical skills. I would then control their fate."

Penelope couldn't believe her ears. How could she have been so gullible? She stared Brutus in the eyes and vowed never to let him win. She'd do whatever it took to help her father recover. She needed to find Cloud and help her get the remedy their father so desperately needed.

Cloud paced back and forth beside the huge boulders strewn across her path. Just as she was preparing to jump onto the first one, a nearby sound caught her attention. She turned to see a small herd of deer behind her on the trail.

They had heard the terrible news of Plato's illness and were there to help in any way they could.

Plato was not just the herd doctor. He willingly shared his skills and knowledge with all the woodland creatures, saving many a life. They owed him a debt of gratitude and would do anything to help him during his time of need.

"Follow us. We know a safe way around the rocks."

The deer leapt off the side of the trail and entered a dark glade crowded with birch trees. Cloud was right on their heels and much to her surprise, Penelope suddenly appeared behind her.

They made their way carefully through the tricky maze of trees. Many had been toppled over by the massive boulders. Keeping the fast-moving deer in sight, they scrambled up and down through the hazardous terrain. Soon the whole entourage emerged on the far side of the rockslide.

Cloud described the plant she was in search of and a few of the deer knew exactly where to find it. They were off and running again and soon emerged in a small cirque along the north ridge of Crystal Peak.

The deer pointed toward the far edge of the hanging valley. Wasting no time, Cloud raced toward the cliff edge and put her nose to the ground until she could smell the pungent herb, still alive and blooming. She snatched it up and stowed it safely in her carrier.

Now they just needed to get back to the valley before darkness fell and the trip became too treacherous.

As she stood at the edge of the cliff looking up at the darkening sky, an idea took hold. Why not slide down the glacial snow chute at her feet instead of weaving back through the boulder field? It would cut miles, not to mention, precious hours, off the journey.

She yelled a heart-felt, "Thank you!" to the deer, told Penelope she'd meet her back in the valley, and without hesitation stepped over the edge, sliding on all four hooves through the snow. But it was steeper than she realized and she was soon completely out of control.

Just as Cloud was about to topple head over heels, Penelope grabbed her tail in her mouth and steadied her. Between the two of them, leaning and counter balancing each other, they were able to navigate safely down the treacherous shortcut.

They ran full-out through the forest at the base of the chute and were soon racing across Paradise Valley.

The waiting unicorns parted as Cloud and Penelope galloped up. And, there, smack in the middle of the herd was Plato, safe, warm and sleeping soundly.

Cloud gently nuzzled him awake. Fighting his heavy eyelids, he tried to focus on her face. He was far too weak to speak, but a small smile formed on his lips.

Cloud dropped the healing herb in front of Plato and told him to eat it all. He slowly chewed the plant, but the effort became too much and he fell back to sleep. Cloud kept nuzzling him to no avail. It was now up to the herb and her father's strength.

Cloud and Penelope stayed by his side all through the night. At first light, Cloud went to collect some creek water for the three of them. Upon her return, she was delighted to see her father gingerly standing with Penelope's help. He drank heartily and sat back on his haunches, exhausted, but happy.

Penelope confessed to the whole sordid mess and tearfully apologized. She said she would understand if Plato never wanted to see her again, but he would have nothing of it. She had helped save him, after all, and had hopefully learned a valuable lesson. Greed and selfishness will eventually collect their dues. What matters most is your willingness to help others in their time of need.

Only time would tell if Penelope had learned this lesson.

Chapter 2

It had been a week since Cloud's fateful birthday party and what should have been the start of her training to be herd healer.

Plato had fully recovered from the cassava root poisoning, thanks to Cloud's quick thinking and some help from the remorseful Penelope.

Life was returning to normal in Paradise Valley. Cloud's ceremony would take place today, and this time everyone was keeping a close eye on Penelope.

But, on this day, Penelope was the least of their worries; for in the neighboring valley, Brutus was finalizing plans of his own.

Years before, Brutus' father, Dante, had ruled over the unicorns of Paradise Valley. He was a harsh, merciless ruler with no patience for weakness of any kind. Herd members were exiled for the smallest of transgressions – including being sick. The herd lived in constant fear.

One young herd member, Plato, was disheartened by what he witnessed and vowed to help those who were thrown out of the valley during their time of greatest need. He secretly studied all the plants in the area and tested their properties on himself.

He began to collect the herbs needed to create his own tinctures. As soon as his small pharmacy was ready, he snuck the life-saving medicine to the exiled herd members.

His amazing knowledge and great compassion didn't go unnoticed and he soon had a very loyal following, not just among the exiled, but also their friends and family in Paradise Valley.

They say that no good deed goes unpunished, and soon Dante caught wind of what Plato was doing.

Dante hated the thought of someone else having any influence over the herd. He had to put a stop to it, so he set out to discredit Plato in front of the herd. This way Dante could exile him and take ownership of the plant pharmacy. He would do this using a plant of his own.

As a young colt, Dante had eaten some hawthorn bark. It was during the great drought and grass was scarce. Unbeknownst to him, hawthorn bark is very poisonous to unicorns.

His mother had saved his life by feeding him witch-hazel, but Dante was never the same again. He had become angry and short-tempered.

This miserable episode from his childhood gave him an idea on how to deal with Plato - a diabolical idea. He would sprinkle hawthorn bark on the herd's favorite grazing spots and blame the inevitable sickness on Plato and his 'dangerous' pharmacy. He would then dole out witch-hazel and save everyone.

The grateful unicorns would all agree that Plato had to go and that Dante was the only one to trust.

Fortunately for the herd, Plato knew all too well what hawthorn bark looked like and what it could do to a unicorn. That was how he was able to stop Dante.

Plato was up early each morning collecting the freshest of newly blossomed flowers.

On this particular morning, he couldn't help but notice that Dante was also out in the forest early. Plato was well hidden in a flowering shrub, and Dante had no idea he was just a few feet away. He had a perfect view of Dante carefully pulling strips of hawthorn bark off a tree.

Curious and confused, Plato followed Dante back to the valley, only to witness him scattering the bark about. Plato yelled at some unsuspecting young unicorns as they were about to start grazing.

Dante jumped at the sound of Plato's voice and, in a panic, bolted through the valley. The bewildered herd watched him run past, the toxic bark spewing from his carrier.

As a crowd gathered, Plato quickly explained the dangerous situation. Everyone chipped in to collect and destroy any remnants of the dangerous hawthorn.

Needless to say, a unanimous decision was made to exile Dante and return all the unjustly exiled unicorns back to Paradise Valley.

Dante hadn't been heard from since. But Dante's son, Brutus, became leader of the neighboring herd and had a grudge to settle with Plato. He swore he would avenge his father and regain his family's rightful place as rulers of Paradise Valley.

This brings us back to Cloud's big ceremony. Everyone was in a festive mood. The weather was sunny and warm, food was plentiful, and everyone was happy that their beloved Cloud would finally have her day.

Brutus was counting on the Paradise Valley herd being in a charitable mood, as he made his way toward the huge crowd gathered around Cloud and Plato. He feigned humbleness and regret for the calamity on Cloud's birthday, for he was sure they were all well aware of his part in the cassava incident. He then set down a beautiful arrangement of fresh flowers, explaining that it was a token of his remorse and repentance.

An awkward silence followed as the herd watched Cloud and Plato, anxious to see their reaction.

Plato was sure that even Brutus wasn't brazen enough to walk into the middle of their herd with malicious intentions. Maybe he really did want to make amends.

The flowers looked harmless enough. So in a gesture of good faith, Plato scooped up a big mouthful of the delicious-looking flowers and chewed away.

A gasp could be heard from the crowd, but when Plato smiled and said, "Wonderful!" with no apparent ill-effects, the herd let out a sigh of relief and joined him.

Brutus couldn't have been happier or more shocked at their naivety. Gullibility obviously ran in the family, just look at what Penelope had fallen for last week.

The hawthorn bark was torn into very thin strips; woven between the flower stems, it was nearly imperceptible. The awful effects should show themselves any minute now.

As soon as the herd was reeling from the toxin, Brutus would alert his trusted advisors and together they would run Plato and his weakened herd out of Paradise Valley. Actually, the sickened herd would have to go – the only place with enough of the cure for all of them was in Brutus' valley.

Witch-hazel was piled at the far end of the valley, so they would have to leave immediately if they wanted to get to it in time. So deliciously diabolical.

There was just one problem with his plan. Brutus had left the hawthorn bark shredding to his most trusted friend, Hank. Hank didn't want to touch such a dangerous plant and, therefore, passed the job on to the only herd member he could convince to do it - the densest herd member - Gart.

Gart, who nervously focused solely on impressing Brutus, mixed up the two plants. He thoroughly shredded the witch-hazel into the flower bouquet and carefully piled the hawthorn bark at the edge of the valley.

So while Brutus waited impatiently for Plato's herd to start showing signs of discomfort, his own unsuspecting herd came upon the carefully laid-out hawthorn bark. Not knowing what it was and thinking it was set out for them, they decided to give it a try.

Just as Brutus was realizing his plan was taking much too long to unfold, he heard a scream from across Paradise Valley. It seemed to come from his valley. He turned and galloped toward the sound.

As he breathlessly entered his valley, he saw the carnage that hawthorn bark can impart. Most of his herd was lying in the grass, groaning and rolling side to side.

Brutus' advisors had heard the groans while waiting for Brutus' signal. They all stood there helplessly, not knowing what was happening. But Brutus had an inkling. He saw the remnants of hawthorn bark on the ground. He grabbed Hank by the mane and spun him around.

"What did you do?" he screamed!

"It was Gart. I gave the job to Gart," Hank moaned, as he cowered before Brutus.

Gart had gone down to the creek to wash all the bark out of his coat and decided he had earned a nice nap in the shade. He, therefore, missed all the fateful goings-on, but would soon face the wrath of Brutus and certain exile.

If the hawthorn bark was here, Brutus was able to deduce where the witch-hazel was.

Plato and his herd had unwittingly eaten the flower bouquet and, with it, the cure for hawthorn bark poisoning. That bouquet held every bit of witch-hazel Brutus was able to find.

Cloud and Plato had followed Brutus back to his valley and now stood wondering what had befallen the poor unicorns there.

Unwilling to let them know of his malicious plan, Brutus explained that his herd seemed to have accidentally eaten hawthorn bark and that there was no witch-hazel in the vicinity.

Plato and Cloud were no dummies. They had both recognized the witch-hazel in the flower bouquet. It had reminded Plato that he'd been meaning to replenish his own stores of it. It didn't take them long to figure out there had been a mix-up on Brutus' part - a lucky mix-up for their herd, but not for Brutus'.

Instead of fretting over what could have been, Plato and Cloud got to work discussing where the nearest witch-hazel could be found.

It was a very rare plant, not to mention, it was the end of its growing season and only fresh witch-hazel would work. Things were looking bleak.

"There's only one answer," said Cloud. "I have to pay a visit to Leonardo."

"That's too dangerous!" exclaimed Plato. "I can't let you do it."

Without hesitating, Cloud smiled bravely at her father, spun and galloped toward the forest.

"There's no other way and no time to argue," she shouted as she sped across the valley toward Lolo Peak.

Plato knew there was nothing to do but wish her well.

As Cloud raced into the forest, Leonardo stood in his cave near the craggy summit of Lolo Peak, shaking his head.

Being over 100 years old had given him much wisdom, but the ability to see the future was a gift he was born with and sometimes regretted having.

Those foolish youngsters, he thought to himself, always plotting and struggling for power. When would they learn? He blamed every unicorn for the vices of a few, reasoning that the best of them, if they were truly noble, would have a positive influence on the others.

He obviously didn't know everything.

The potion for hawthorn bark poisoning, without the use of witch-hazel, was complicated and intricate. He wasn't sure he was feeling up to the challenge.

But this young unicorn, Cloud, had much potential. Maybe he should give her a role in the creation of the potion. She appeared to have the capability to become his apprentice, his one and only apprentice - a job coveted by many through the years. He had kept his eye on this girl for some time, waiting for her to grow up. Now she was on her way to him.

Meanwhile, back in Brutus' valley, Penelope weighed her options. She knew that Cloud was taking a huge risk by asking Leonardo for help. He was known for his legendary impatience with fools. He felt it his obligation to teach them a lesson. If they offended or disappointed him, they were unceremoniously turned into bats.

Leonardo loved bats. They ate the annoying bugs that kept him awake at night. The more bats in the world, the better. So, if you were ill-suited for anything else, you could at least eat bugs, Leonardo reasoned.

He wasn't totally heartless though. The imbeciles only had to work as a bat for a month or two, depending on how offended he was. Sometimes friends or family could make a heartfelt case for their bat loved ones, and he'd release them early, but their case had to be very convincing.

All of this is, of course, untrue. Family members only thought their loved ones were turned into bats because when they visited the cave and shouted the names of their family members, bats would fly out of the entrance in their stead.

In actuality, Leonardo offered these slower-witted students an intense course in flora, medicinal properties, and common sense. These students studied night and day in the back rooms of the cave and were often some of his best graduates.

He kept the bat myth alive to keep students on their best behavior.

Penelope, believing the bat myth, had an idea. If Cloud were to upset Leonardo and get turned into a bat for a few months, that would give Penelope plenty of time to ingratiate herself with her father and the herd. If Penelope could make Cloud look really bad, Cloud would be shamed for life. Maybe she'd even be too ashamed to show her face in Paradise Valley again. Hmmmm, this could work.

Penelope quietly snuck away, as Plato helped the sick unicorns.

Cloud was nearing Leonardo's cave just as the last rays of the sun lit the path. She stopped in front of the entrance and called out a greeting. Nothing stirred, but Cloud knew to wait patiently. Any stomping or shouting would be unwise.

Suddenly, Leonardo appeared in the entrance.

"What took you so long?" he muttered. "Come, I've got a few of the ingredients for hawthorn bark ingestion ready to go. You will have to gather the rest of them."

Cloud stared at him with wide eyes. No one had ever been allowed to work on a potion with Leonardo. He was known for his perfectionism.

"WELL? Are you up for the task or not?" he said, much too loudly.

"I...I...ummm. Yes - I am," Cloud managed to stammer.

"We will be needing blue juniper and milk thistle."

Cloud nodded slowly, unsure of what he expected from her. It was getting darker by the second.

"Well, get out there. Time is of the essence!" Leonardo shouted.

With her heart racing, Cloud spun around and started back down the steep path.

Did he really expect her to find those plants in the dark? They were hard enough to find in broad daylight. But she knew it was either find the plants or develop a taste for bugs. She got to work.

Penelope was just a few zigzags down from the cave when she overheard the exchange between Leonardo and Cloud.

This was perfect. Cloud would never find those plants in the dark, and Penelope would have fun making sure of it.

She started by piling rocks on the trail. A few scary noises would soon be in order. Maybe a fallen tree to block the trail would be a nice touch. This was going to be so easy. But just as she reached her neck out to grab a tree, she slipped in the loose dirt on the steep edge of the trail and found herself toppling end over end down the mountainside. She screamed in alarm.

As Cloud continued down the steep trail, she planned her mission. Milk thistle was very rare in these mountains, it would take time to find. But on her way up, Cloud had noticed a blue juniper growing along the trail. As she carefully made her way to its location, she was startled by a piercing scream. The plants would have to wait. She turned toward the scream.

It was too dark to make anything out, so she would have to rely on sounds. She stood still and listened, her ears forward. As she tilted her head in different directions, she thought she could hear a faint voice breaking through the black stillness. She moved toward the sound.

"Cloud, carefully make your way straight down the slope near the large stump," came an eerie, yet familiar voice.

Cloud found the stump and started cautiously down the slope. She heard a soft moan and there was Penelope a few feet downhill from her. She rushed to her side and carefully helped her to her feet.

"I saw Mom, Cloud. She was here with me," said Penelope softly.

"Don't be ridiculous, Penelope. Mom left us years ago. Why would she be here? What are you doing here?"

"I came to help you, but I made a mess of it, I'm afraid," Penelope sighed, as she wobbled back and forth.

Cloud checked her for injuries and finding none, decided to find a safe place for Penelope to lie down and wait while she collected the plants. As Cloud studied the area for a flat spot, the moon peeked out from behind the clouds and shone on a beautiful patch of milk thistle. Cloud stared in disbelief.

After making sure Penelope was safe, Cloud snatched up the milk thistle and quickly found the blue juniper she'd seen earlier. She was back in the cave in no time.

Leonardo couldn't believe his eyes. This girl was more amazing than he realized.

He quickly mixed Cloud's leafs with the secret ingredients he'd gathered from his enormous collection - carefully arranged on rock shelves that seemed to go on for miles.

The cure was soon ready and he sent Cloud down the mountain with it. There wasn't a second to waste.

Cloud galloped full out, jumping and sliding down the treacherous trail. She quickly found Plato and they began to give out the potion to each member of Brutus' sickened herd.

When all the unicorns had been administered to, they sent Hank up the mountain to help Penelope down.

Before long the herd members were back on their feet and looking much improved and more than a little grateful.

With tragedy averted and Hank and Penelope safely back in the valley, this had all the trappings of a happy ending, but at the edge of the forest a pair of menacing emerald eyes watched the happenings closely.

Chapter 3

Leonardo stood at the edge of the cliff, staring into the dark forest below. He knew, of course, that Cloud was successful in helping Brutus' herd. He only wished he could somehow change the future he was foreseeing.

Events would not go well for Cloud, and if he could, he would alter them. But some things were out of his control.

He turned to look at the beautiful, dapple grey unicorn standing next to him. Perhaps, between the two of them . . .

Down in the valley below, Dante stayed hidden at the edge of the forest, watching. His piercing, emerald eyes never leaving his son.

How would Brutus convince his weakened herd that he could watch over them and keep them safe after the ordeal he'd just put them through?

Then that meddling Cloud became their hero, making Brutus look even worse. Brutus was good at spinning things in his favor, but Dante was prepared to step in and help his son if necessary. For now, he would lay low and see how events transpired.

The next morning in Paradise Valley, Cloud and Penelope were up early discussing their ordeal on the mountain.

"You really didn't see Mom?" Penelope asked. "She was there, I know it. I could feel her watching over me."

"Penelope, you were hurt and scared, of course you wanted your mom to be with you, but you have to face the fact that she's gone," Cloud replied caringly.

"How do you explain the voice we both heard?" Penelope asked.

"It had to be Leonardo conjuring up some of his magic to help us," explained Cloud. "Now enough of this nonsense, we have work to do. First off, we need to go check on Brutus' herd."

After consulting with Plato, Cloud gathered some beneficial herbs to share with the recovering unicorns and, with Penelope by her side, started off through the forest.

As they walked down the path leading out of Paradise Valley, they heard twigs snapping up ahead. Cloud stopped and listened, but all was silent. As they continued on, they heard rustling coming from all directions.

Suddenly a huge black unicorn appeared out of nowhere. He reared up, his front hooves thrashing at the air. They could feel the power in his massive legs as they backed away from his gigantic flailing hooves.

"Your help is no longer needed," he shouted. "I think it wise you stay in your own valley".

And with that he was gone.

Cloud and Penelope stared in shock. Who was he? Why would he say that?

Penelope, having seen enough, fearfully galloped back toward Paradise Valley, but Cloud remained in place. She was free to come and go as she saw fit. No stranger was going to stop her from doing what she knew was right. She fearlessly continued down the trail to help the weakened unicorns.

Her help was greatly appreciated by Brutus' herd. They were shaken up by the accidental hawthorn poisoning and needed to be looked after and reassured. Cloud spent the day going from one unicorn to another, asking how they felt and explaining the many herbs she'd brought along for them to try.

As darkness fell, Cloud realized she'd lost track of time and needed to be on her way home. She bid everyone farewell and started down the path through the forest. She was nearly halfway home, when she heard a familiar rustling. As she spun around, the gigantic black unicorn appeared.

"It is quite apparent you didn't heed my warning. I'm afraid I can't let you get away with that," he snarled.

As Cloud defiantly stood her ground, trying to stop shaking, a dapple grey unicorn appeared at her side, snorting and rearing.

"How dare you threaten my daughter?" yelled the beautiful unicorn as she stomped her front hooves on the ground. "Leave now or Leonardo and I will make you sorry you didn't."

At the mention of Leonardo's name, Dante snorted loudly and turned to go, but not before issuing a warning to Cloud.

"I'll be watching you."

With that he was gone.

Cloud stared at the dapple grey, trying to calm her racing heart.

"Mom?"

"Come. There's no time to chat. I have to get you home," commanded the dapple grey, as she turned and galloped toward Paradise Valley.

Cloud stood frozen in shock. After shaking her head, trying to clear it, she quickly followed her mother, Calypso, through the forest. They stopped near the entrance to the valley and Calypso spun around.

"You're safe now. I have some unfinished business to take care of with our friend, Dante," she shouted as she hurried back into the dark forest.

Cloud couldn't believe her ears. Dante! He was infamous in their valley. Cloud and Penelope grew up hearing scary stories starring Dante. He was the stuff of nightmares and he was here. She took off at a gallop after her mom.

Penelope had spent the day telling everyone about her encounter with a treacherous, gigantic, black unicorn. In her version, she saved the valley from this scary intruder by chasing him away. It was much later that she realized Cloud hadn't returned to the valley with her.

It was quickly getting dark and Plato was concerned. Knowing Penelope's nature, he asked for the truth about this black unicorn.

Alexander Boden Photo

Meanwhile, Dante sulked in the shadows of the age old ponderosas, waiting for the inevitable appearance of Calypso. She would never let this go. He had promised to stay away from his old home, but Brutus needed his help.

Brutus deserved to be the leader of Paradise Valley. Something Dante had been robbed of. He had only returned to help his son capture what he, himself, had lost.

He heard her thundering hoof beats bearing down on him. How did she always know exactly where he was? Was this part of Leonardo's training?

"You failed to honor your promise," Calypso whispered harshly as she slid to a stop in front of Dante. He could feel her trying to control her anger, something Leonardo had no doubt taught her.

"My dear, I've told you I will do anything for my child. You seem to know the feeling," Dante said with a sneer.

"After you spread that chamomile over our pasture. . .we were all so groggy. Then you had your thugs sneak up on either side of me to carry me far away from my family, forcing me to become a part of your herd, just to get back at Plato . . . I cannot and will not, ever forgive you. If I hadn't escaped and been found by Leonardo - wandering in the forest, weak, lost and alone . . . I owe him my life," Calypso held back the tears as she spoke. "Now you're back to cause more trouble! How dare you?!"

"Oh, come now, don't be so melodramatic! It wasn't as bad as all that. You could have been my queen! Don't you see what we could have created together? Making you work twice as hard as the other unicorns, with half the food, was my way of persuading you to rethink things, but you were too stubborn. Not my fault," Dante shouted bitterly.

"You have no idea the hurt you have caused my family. They thought I had abandoned them for you! I can never return to Paradise Valley," her anger was rising again. She took a deep breath and stared Dante square in the eyes.

"Get away from my family and don't you ever come back," she said calmly.

They both heard the rustling in the trees behind them. Thinking the thugs were back, Calypso spun around and lunged toward the sound, only to come face to face with Cloud.

"Mom, I . . . we . . . had no idea. I'm so sorry for what you went through," sputtered Cloud through her tears. Her obvious anguish kept Calypso from being angry with her for following.

While mother and daughter were busy with their sentimental hogwash, Dante saw his chance to strike out. He reared up, only to be hit in the head by a huge pine branch held firmly in Plato's mouth.

As he staggered back in shock, Dante was confronted by Plato and Penelope, neither of whom looked happy to see him. Knowing he was bested, Dante lunged into the darkened forest and disappeared. For the time being.

Plato, Calypso, Cloud and Penelope stood staring at each other in the dark clearing.

"Thank you for protecting Cloud," Plato finally broke the silence, trying to get over his shock at seeing Calypso.

"We heard everything. I am so sorry! We had no idea. All the rumors Dante spread . . . they were so believable and so devastating. But you're back now," he managed to say as he choked back his tears. "Cloud's induction ceremony is in the morning. You and Leonardo will make the celebration complete!"

With that, the joyfully reunited family started back toward their Paradise Valley home, blissfully unaware that Dante was on his way up the mountain to pay a visit to Leonardo.

Somebody had to pay for this.

Book 2

Chiron Enchants

Chapter 1

Even the fiery sun seemed content as it rose over Paradise Valley. After too many years away, Calypso had finally returned home. After a sleepless night of non-stop questions for their long-lost mom, Cloud's family was happy and whole again.

Today was also the day of Cloud's much delayed ceremony. She would officially begin her training to become the herd healer.

As soon as it was light enough, a messenger was sent to Lolo Peak to invite Leonardo, the sage, to this very special ceremony. When they hadn't returned by mid-morning, it was apparent something was amiss. The crowd was getting restless, and Cloud's family was getting worried. They had kept the events of the day before to themselves so as not to worry the herd. And, with Dante back, there was plenty to worry about.

Penelope couldn't have been happier about the delay in Cloud's stupid, unfair ceremony. She realized this snafu was a wonderful opportunity to see the whole affair cancelled. As the rest of the family paced and worried, she stared at the trail leading up to Leonardo's cave, formulating a plan.

"Don't worry! I'll get to the bottom of this," she shouted, galloping toward the trail.

Gart stood at the edge of the forest watching Penelope gallop toward him.   He had no doubt she was up to no good. Gart knew a good heart from a bad one.

He knew a lot of things he wasn't given credit for. He knew the difference between hawthorn bark and witch-hazel, for instance. He also knew he loved Cloud and would never let anyone harm her. It was worth being exiled from Brutus' herd to save her and her herd from the pain of hawthorn bark poisoning. His only regret was that he hadn't hidden the hawthorn bark well enough.

He still had no idea how Brutus' herd found it in the bushes at the far edge of their valley.

Gart, whose real name is Chiron, was one of Leonardo's top students. Born in a far-away valley, he was a standout from birth with his snow-white body and jet-black mane and tail. But Chiron wasn't only unique looking, he was also extremely intelligent.

His parents were approached by Leonardo when Chiron was quite young, asking if they'd let him travel to Lolo Peak to become his student. They immediately agreed. This invitation was an incredible honor.

During his study breaks, Chiron would explore the surrounding valleys. During one of these outings, on a cold, rainy day, he saw Cloud for the first time.

Looking back on that day he realized it wasn't just her magnificent, crystal-white coat or her stunning violet eyes that drew him to her, it was her courage and toughness. He had watched in awe as she scrambled over slippery boulders and down a steep, muddy slope to help a very frightened colt who had gotten lost in the dark, stormy woods. She was so comforting and careful with the colt, her compassion so apparent, that it was love at first sight for Chiron.

Near the end of Chiron's training, Leonardo got word of Brutus' rise to power in a nearby valley. Leonardo was well aware of Brutus' mean streak and knew he needed to keep Brutus in check. He asked Chiron to secretly join Brutus' herd and report back to him if anything looked amiss.

By changing his name to Gart and acting the fool, Chiron could be constantly underfoot with no one noticing him and, more importantly, with no one suspecting he was a spy. He was often given jobs no one else wanted, like shredding poisonous hawthorn bark and hiding it in a bouquet of flowers.

On the morning of Cloud's ceremony, as Chiron watched Penelope draw nearer, he thought back to the night before. He had watched from his hiding place in the forest as Dante had also galloped toward Lolo Peak. Chiron knew exactly where Dante was going after his demeaning confrontation with Plato. So, knowing a little about Dante's temper, Chiron took a shortcut up the mountain, easily beating him to Leonardo's cave. He wanted to warn his beloved teacher about this uninvited guest.

Chiron needn't have worried, for Leonardo had foreseen the looming confrontation and was quite prepared. To Chiron's surprise, Leonardo had set out a banquet of fresh herbs.

"What's all this?" Chiron asked in bewilderment.

"It is a mystic's way of calming a dangerous situation or, in this case, calming a dangerous, and very grumpy, unicorn," answered Leonardo with a smile.

In a matter of moments they heard Dante's thundering hoof beats. Leonardo calmly made his way to the cave entrance to welcome his guest.

Pawing the dirt on the narrow cliff outside Leonardo's cave, Dante's flaring nostrils looked like they were spewing columns of billowing smoke in the cold night air. His horrible temper had reached the boiling point.

Leonardo was completely unruffled as he invited Dante in for a chat and a snack. The snack consisting of as many calming herbs as he could find on his shelves.

Dante, not trusting Leonardo, initially refused the herbs, but after watching Leonardo and his familiar-looking student eat with abandon, he realized he was famished and joined in. He was soon feeling much calmer and somewhat sleepy.

With Dante's very volatile temper subsiding, Leonardo felt they could talk things out in a peaceful manner. Dante had other plans. With a quick lunge, he grabbed Leonardo's mane firmly in his mouth. He then slowly twisted his head downward until Leonardo was laying at his feet. Chiron could only watch in horror, not wanting to provoke Dante further.

Dante placed one of his gigantic hooves on Leonardo's side, holding him firmly in place.

"Did you honestly think you could put me to sleep with your feeble concoction? I am so much stronger than you know. I am invincible and you, my friend, are a meddler," Dante roared at Leonardo.

Just then a strange thing happened. Dante started to stagger backward. He had to take his hoof off of Leonardo to catch himself.

Chiron took this opportunity to lunge at Dante, knocking him over on his side. Now the tables were turned, as Leonardo calmly got to his feet and put his hoof on Dante's huge, muscular neck, firmly holding him in place.

"Are you quite finished with your egotistical rant? We need to have a serious talk. You treated Calypso abysmally, kidnapping her, then starving her half to death. Now you want to harm her daughter. Well, I'm afraid I can't let you do that," sighed Leonardo.

Dante snorted angrily and squirmed feebly under Leonardo's weight.

"Here's what I'm thinking. You go back to your herd right now and never ever show your despicable face in Paradise Valley or on Lolo Peak again. Deal?" Leonardo growled, leaning close to Dante's face.

With that, Leonardo stepped aside and let Dante struggle to his feet.

"Don't assume this is the end of this," snarled Dante.

"GET OUT!" roared Leonardo.

Dante jumped in alarm and stumbled toward the entrance, disappearing into the night.

Chiron followed Dante down the mountain to make sure he actually left, but also to make sure he made it down safely. The herb dinner he ate was obviously quite potent. Leonardo never wished harm on another creature and taught all his students the same philosophy.

Early the next morning, Leonardo was fast asleep in the back of the cave as Chiron quietly left to collect some fresh herbs to replenish the stores.

He met Plato's messenger coming up the trail and heard all about Cloud's ceremony. Explaining that Leonardo had had a long night, he asked the messenger to please wait at the cave entrance until Leonardo awoke. He was quite certain that Leonardo would insist upon feeding the messenger one of his famous healthy breakfasts, so it could be awhile before they arrived back at Paradise Valley. This would give Chiron time to wander down to the valley in hopes of catching a glimpse of Cloud.

He caught a glimpse of Penelope instead and decided to intercept her as she entered the forest. Maybe he could thwart any malicious plans she might have.

Penelope slid to a stop when he stepped out of the thick forest squarely in the middle of her path.

"Oh! Hello? Wait. . .you're part of Brutus' herd, aren't you? I'm . . . was. . . a friend of his," Penelope stammered.

Chiron knew exactly why Penelope was 'friends' with Brutus. He'd overheard the whole sorted story not long after he joined Brutus' herd. Penelope had attempted to take over as herd healer by secretly making Plato, her own father, sick. At that point, her ill-conceived plan was to miraculously cure him. It was a horrible idea that completely backfired. Blinded by envy, she made the mistake of trusting Brutus. Another horrible idea. If Cloud hadn't intervened, who knows what would have happened to Plato.

Having little to no respect for Penelope, Chiron just shrugged his muscular shoulders in answer to her question.

Since the conversation seemed to be over, Penelope tried to push past him on the trail. He blocked her path again.

"And where would you be going on this lovely morning?" he said cheerfully, hoping to get some idea of what her plans were.

"That is definitely none of your business, but if you must know, I am on my way to check on Leonardo. He is late for a very important ceremony," she said with contempt dripping from each word.

A chill ran along Chiron's spine.

"I'd be happy to accompany you on this mission," he managed to say with a smile.

"No need," she huffed as she forcefully pushed past him.

He watched until she disappeared around the next bend, then he set out through the huge cedar trees that lined the trail, quietly following her, unnoticed.

What neither of them knew, was Dante and Brutus were also on their way up Lolo Peak with revenge on their minds. And if Leonardo hadn't foreseen the whole sorted incident, it could have gotten ugly.

Fortunately, Leonardo had figured out exactly what needed to be done. So, just as soon as he finished feeding the hungry messenger a healthy breakfast, he prepared for his upcoming, unhappy guests.

When the hungry messenger had swallowed his last bite, Leonardo told the him to take a secret, well-hidden path down the mountain to Paradise Valley. He assured him he'd be right along - not wanting to hold up the big ceremony any longer than absolutely necessary. He was, of course, counting that healthy breakfast as absolutely necessary. And dealing with Dante once and for all was quite necessary, as well.

As Dante and Brutus drew nearer to Leonardo's cave, they heard hoof beats on the path below them. Quickly hiding in a thick bush on the side of the trail, they waited to see who was coming. As Penelope rounded the corner, Dante jumped into her path.

"I'm afraid you're not welcome here. You better turn around while you still can," he growled menacingly.

Penelope was so startled by his sudden appearance and threatening words, she skidded off the side of the trail and started sliding helplessly down the steep slope.

Dante watched her helplessly flailing to regain her footing as she slid faster and faster down the mountain face.

"She decided to take a shortcut. Smart girl," Dante chuckled as he started back up the trail with Brutus close behind.

Chiron was also watching Penelope. He was far enough away to have to gallop full-out to reach her. He timed his leap perfectly to intercept her fall and save her from a broken leg or worse. They slid to a stop and Penelope stood frozen in shock, staring down the mountain face, realizing the horrible possibilities Chiron helped her avoid.

Cloud watched from the trail below as Penelope and Chiron caught their breath on the steep slope. She had been on her way to find Penelope and witnessed the whole sordid affair. Dante was apparently back with a vengeance, and who was that mysterious unicorn who just saved her sister's life?

"Penelope, are you okay?" she shouted as she galloped toward them.

"I'm fine, thanks to whoever this guy is," panted Penelope. They both looked at Chiron, who smiled sheepishly.

"I'm one of Leonardo's graduates. I was part of Brutus' herd for a short time. . . at Leonardo's request," Chiron said to help fill in their blank stares.

He realized that Cloud never saw him on the day of the hawthorn bark debacle. He had stopped to wash up in the creek on his way back to Leonardo's cave and, thinking quickly, he pretended to be napping when he heard Brutus approaching from his visit to Paradise Valley. Cloud hadn't seen him, and since Brutus immediately threw him out of the herd, she couldn't have seen him on her visit the next day either.

"We can do formal introductions later, right now we need to check on Leonardo," Cloud said worriedly.

The three of them spun in unison and galloped straight up the side of the mountain. A few minutes later, foaming with sweat and completely out of breath, the three of them barged into Leonardo's cave. Expecting the worst, they couldn't believe their eyes.

Leonardo, Dante and Brutus were sitting back on their haunches, laughing and chatting. It could have been afternoon tea, as relaxed and happy as they all looked.

"Well, hello young ones," laughed Leonardo. "What brings you here on this fine and glorious day? Shouldn't you be preparing for the big ceremony?"

"We were worried about you, since. . . because. . .," stammered Chiron, staring from Leonardo to Dante and back again.

"No need! It turns out, Dante was in desperate need of my help and none of us realized it. As soon as he arrived this morning, I asked him a few questions that had been bothering me. After listening carefully to his answers, I figured out what has been making him miserable all these years. It was that nasty hawthorn bark he ate as a colt. He was never able to purge it from his system. He just needed some blue juniper elixir with a touch of slippery elm and, viola, good as new," explained Leonardo.

With that Dante stood up and, with a very serious look on his face, apologized profusely to everyone present, including Brutus. It appeared Brutus wanted off the hook for his transgressions by putting all the blame on his dad.

Cloud wasn't buying that one.

Chapter 2

Cloud's induction ceremony was perfect. Everyone she loved and cared about was there, including Chiron, her newest friend. Luckily, the whole ceremony went off without a hitch and the time for merry-making had begun. Cloud politely touched muzzles with all the well-wishers, but her thoughts kept returning to Chiron. He was extremely fascinating.

Cloud's mind kept returning to the walk back from Leonardo's. Cloud and Chiron enjoyed a non-stop, relaxing, interesting, funny, educational conversation. By the time they reached the valley floor, their bond was sealed. They would be in each other's lives from this time forward. It was an unspoken, fully understood truth.

Penelope had followed them down the mountain and couldn't help noticing how perfectly suited they were. Their genuine laughter, the intense looks, the well-put questions and deep answers. It was enough to make her sick. Cloud had all the luck. She would soon become herd healer, Penelope's dream job, and now she finds true love. It was more than Penelope could bear to think about. Surely she could find a way to put a stop to all this nonsense.

After the   ceremony, as Penelope's devious mind wandered over various malicious plans, her eyes settled on Dante and Brutus. They had been invited here by Cloud after Dante's brave and sincere apology. It was strange having them here after their abysmal behavior. As if reading her mind, Brutus looked her way. He slowly approached and nodded in greeting.

"What a wonderful day," he said with a sickeningly slow smile.

"Yes, quite," Penelope answered, not even trying to hide the sarcasm.

Was he serious? Had he really changed his ways? Her answer came as she studied his eyes. She could see the simmering anger just below the surface. He nudged her toward a group of trees.

Once out of view of the masses, he opened up with his true feelings.

"Okay, I can understand you hating me after I betrayed you, but hear me out. I had to sabotage your plan to become herd healer. It would have been too obvious to everyone. You would have been exiled. The way it played out, you could blame it all on me and come out smelling like a rose. I did it for your own good," he said in a vain attempt at sincerity.

Penelope knew better, but decided to see how this would all play out. Brutus could be the answer to Cloud's undoing.

"Oh, I see what you're saying," she said, while staring demurely at the ground. "You only had my best interest at heart. I guess I owe you my thanks".

She had to keep looking down so as not to show her disgust. Two could play this sorted game of deception.

"No thanks necessary, but you can help me with two, little, nagging problems. Cloud and Chiron. She has meddled with and humiliated my family for the last time. And, speaking of meddling and humiliating, Chiron was obviously working with Leonardo to spy on me," he said angrily, his voice rising as his true feelings boiled over.

This was perfect. It looked like luck was finally on Penelope's side. She'd get Brutus to do all the dirty work while she innocently watched. Now, to formulate a plan. She smiled sweetly at Brutus.

Hank stood at the edge of the trees listening to the exchange between Brutus and Penelope. He couldn't believe his ears. Would they never learn? Were their hearts so dark, they couldn't appreciate the good around them? He had to save Penelope. He knew she had to have a grain of goodness left inside her heart and he would find it. She was worth it. He moved closer as he heard Brutus begin to speak again.

"I've heard stories of a far off valley in the shadow of Minaret Peak that is in need of a powerful healer's touch. They are all breathing in ash from a nearby volcano and falling gravely ill. Their healer doesn't have the knowledge to help them, but Cloud just might," said Brutus with a menacing smile. "Rumor has it this volcano could erupt at any moment. Oh, don't look so alarmed. The herd has been convinced to leave the area. They are safe and feeling much improved. But Cloud doesn't know that. It would be so sad to lose a talented healer to such a catastrophe, but a healer, even one in training, signs on for better or worse. And, if this healer brings along a friend. . ."

Hank felt a shiver go along his spine. Brutus was beyond mean. Hank was ashamed to admit he had ever been his trusted advisor. The hawthorn bark incident was beyond Hank's comprehension and he should have tried to stop it. It made him sick to think Brutus would actually stoop that low again. Hank had seen enough. To make up for his stupidity, he felt it his duty to see that Brutus never hurt anyone again and that included Penelope.

Penelope said her goodbyes to Brutus after promising to start laying the ground work for their plan. As she left the hiding place in the trees, she ran into Hank. He looked as startled as she did.

"Oh, hello. Where did you come from?" he said, hoping to look like he'd just arrived and had no idea she'd just been plotting a diabolical scheme with Brutus.

"I was just stretching my legs. It's been a long morning," Penelope said, throwing in a yawn for good measure.

"I'll walk back with you," Hank said. "I was hoping to run into you today."

As they started back toward the crowded meadow, Hank glanced sideways at Penelope. She was so beautiful with her jet black coat and black and white mane and tail. He felt plain in comparison, sporting the same golden coat as so many other unicorns. Sure he shimmered in the right light, but no one was ever looking when it counted, so what good was that.

"You look lovely today. Uhh. . .actually, you're lovely every day...umm. I'm sorry for being so forward," Hank stammered.

Penelope couldn't believe her ears. Her? Lovely? No one had ever told her that. It was always Cloud this and Cloud that. She stopped and turned toward Hank.

He was actually blushing. His cheeks were fiery red under his shimmering coat. She'd never really noticed him. She was always too caught up in her own personal melodramas. Actually, she'd never paid attention to any other unicorns. She only wanted them to pay attention to her.

"Thank you," she said with all sincerity. "I love the way your coat glistens in the sunlight."

Hank blushed even brighter. Someone was finally looking when it counted.

They both smiled shyly at each other and continued back to the party, walking down the path side by side.

The party continued well into the night with prancing and laughter galore. Unicorns from far and wide had journeyed to Paradise Valley to wish Cloud well and to see Calypso again. Everybody was curious about Calypso's long absence and were rightfully astonished by the tale she told.

Even more astonishing was Dante's presence at the ceremony. Calypso's capacity for forgiveness was to be commended. It was very apparent she was in a joyful mood, the way she and Plato were gazing adoringly at each other.

Cloud and Chiron spent the evening getting to know each other better. They talked and laughed for hours. There was a bit of gazing adoringly going on between them, too. It was the perfect end to a perfectly glorious day.

Hank and Penelope also talked late into the night. He confessed that he had overheard her talking to Brutus. He tried to explain to her that Brutus had a dark heart and knew no loyalty. Brutus would find a way to blame her for every awful thing he did. He asked if she was really so jealous of Cloud that she'd want to see harm come to her. Penelope hesitated, tears brimming in her eyes.

"You have no reason to be jealous," he said softly. "You are amazing. I used to see you in the forest while I was out collecting plants. I once saw you teaching young colts and fillies how to forage. You were so patient, yet playful. They loved you.

I've seen you carefully carry a special, rare plant back to your herd so you could share it with everybody. You should never be jealous of anybody. You are special and rare yourself."

Penelope could only smile through the tears. Her frozen heart was starting to melt at last. She had finally found love.

At first light, after a healthy breakfast, everyone said their goodbyes and headed home.

Cloud and Penelope walked with Chiron and Hank to the edge of the valley. Unable or unwilling to say goodbye, they decided to walk them back to their homes. It seemed like a good idea at the time, but they may have rethought it, if they had known what was in store.

Chapter 3

The four of them decided to climb Lolo Peak first. They'd get Chiron safely home and enjoy the glorious views along the way. Besides, Hank was hoping to avoid going back to his valley for as long as possible. He knew he couldn't live under Brutus' rule for another day. But before he left his home for good, he needed to confront Brutus and tell him to leave Cloud and Penelope alone. It would probably get ugly.

For now, they'd just enjoy the beautiful day and the wonderful company. They raced each other, played hide and seek, stopped for delicious foraging opportunities, and told dumb jokes. When they were almost halfway up the mountain, they stopped at Lochsa Falls to take a break.

Hank and Penelope were having so much fun splashing around in the water, Cloud told them to stay and play while she walked Chiron the rest of the way. She actually wanted to spend more time alone with him anyway.

They all said their goodbyes and Cloud and Chiron started up the trail. They were two zig-zags further up the mountain, when Brutus appeared out of nowhere.

"Cloud, I'm so glad I found you," he exclaimed breathlessly. "The unicorns of Minaret Peak are in desperate need of your help. They are breathing dangerous ash from a nearby volcano and are in dire straits. They need a good healer. I can show you the way, but you'll have to come now. There isn't a second to waste. Chiron, I'm sure we could use your help, too."

He spun around in a full circle, stirring up dust with his pawing hooves, while trying to look as worried as he could.

"Please help me," he sobbed. "I really need to make amends after the horrible, hurtful things I let my dad talk me into. I have to make up for my stupidity and prove to my fellow unicorns that I'm not a monster."

He stared at Cloud and Chiron with teary eyes, then reared into the air.

"Let's go!" he yelled, hoping to startle them into action before they could think about it.

But, much to his surprise, Cloud and Chiron were ready and willing to follow him. No questions asked. What a couple of goody two shoes. Brutus rolled his eyes as he spun toward Minaret Peak.

They were off and running across the side of Lolo Peak, cutting their own trail along the steep slope. Each of them stumbled and recovered numerous times as they scrambled over the rocky terrain.

Brutus couldn't believe how easy this was. If these two fools didn't fall off the side of the mountain first, the volcano would do them in soon enough.

His plan was perfect. When they reached the base of the volcano, he'd feign an injury and send them on alone with instructions to find the poor herd of sick unicorns. He'd even throw in a bit about the unicorns hiding in the trees to avoid the ash. These gullible do-gooders would search high and low to find them and, no doubt, would not give up until they did or until it was too late. The only thing Brutus had to worry about was the volcano erupting before they got there, so speed was of the essence.

Meanwhile, Hank and Penelope were napping in the shade of the pines, listening to the rushing water of the falls. It was heavenly. But when they awoke some time later, Cloud still hadn't returned. Just then Leonardo came around the corner at a blistering pace for such an old unicorn.

"Where are Chiron and Cloud?" he barked. "I've had a horrible premonition of them being in trouble."

"Oh no," cried Penelope. "They were on their way to your cave some time ago."

"I saw no sign of them on my way here," said Leonardo. "They must have left the trail, but why?"

Penelope made a startled gasp.

"I think I know exactly why. Brutus! They're headed for Minaret Peak."

"That's why I had lava and ash in my dream," said Leonardo.

Without another word, the three of them bolted toward Minaret Peak. If they hurried, maybe they could get there in time.

Brutus, Cloud and Chiron were foaming with sweat and completely out of breath, when they stopped at the edge of a steep drop-off that ended in a sheer cliff. Minaret Peak was in full view.

They'd made incredible time, and Brutus was ready to give them his well-rehearsed spiel just as soon as he 'tripped' and twisted his leg. First they all needed to catch their breath and take in the magnitude of this huge volcano. It was quite formidable as it belched smoke and ash into the air.

"Oh my, that is unbelievable," panted Cloud, as she stared at the massive, rumbling volcano.

"Yes. What's even more unbelievable are all the poor, sick unicorns living in its shadow, breathing in that poisonous ash as we speak," said Brutus in his most pitiful voice.

He glanced around, looking for a good rock to 'trip' over. When he'd found the perfect stone, he made a very believable show of falling over it while feigning preoccupation with the fate of all those poor unicorns below. He laid on the ground moaning in 'pain'.

"Oh no! This is horrible. I can't walk, but I need to help those poor, helpless souls down there," he cried, conjuring up tears. He was so good at being bad.

"Don't worry. We'll help them. You stay here and rest until you're able to walk again," Cloud said.

Brutus smiled feebly and started his devious spiel about the poor unicorns hiding in the trees below, blah, blah. This was too easy. He was almost to the end of his instructions for their destruction, when he heard hoof beats approaching.

"Wait!" yelled Penelope. "He's lying! The unicorns of Minaret Peak are safe. He's telling you this story because he wants revenge. He wants you two down there when the volcano erupts. He thought I was his partner in this plan. He expects me to help convince you to go. He believes this because I have been a horrible, selfish idiot. He knew I was willing to stoop very low to get my way, but I'm done with that. I was wrong and so is he!"

Everyone stood, wide-eyed, frozen in shock. Penelope stood firmly in place with tears running down her face. Her true beauty was finally shining through. The beauty Hank knew was there all along. He slowly put his head over her neck and nuzzled her, letting out a deep sigh.

The spell was broken when Brutus screamed in protest and lunged at Cloud and Chiron. He had purposely chosen this particular place to stop. He needed a very precarious drop-off nearby, just in case he had to resort to Plan B. Well, here came Plan B in all its glory.

Cloud was watching Brutus closely after Penelope's speech, so she was able to react when he lunged. Chiron, unfortunately, was not and took the full brunt of Brutus' weight.

The force of the blow sent Chiron reeling sideways down the steep slope, the cliff edge a short distance away. His legs were facing uphill so he had no way of slowing himself down. Momentum and gravity were working together to cause him to slide even faster.

Cloud wasted no time. She jumped down the slope as far as she could and as soon as her hooves hit the ground, she lunged up into the air again. She was below Chiron in an instant. She swung around and put her head against his back while bracing her legs beneath her. Her hooves were digging deep trenches into the ground until she and Chiron finally slid to a stop inches from the drop-off. Behind her, Cloud could hear rocks falling and bouncing down the cliff face. It seemed like it took each rock forever to reach the ground far below.

Jeremiah LaRocco

As soon as they'd recovered from the shock of Brutus' attack, Penelope and Hank started down the slope to help Cloud and Chiron. But, just as they reached Chiron, the ground gave way under Cloud's back legs.

Cloud's chest slammed into the cliff face as she pawed frantically with her front legs to gain a hold. Chiron froze in place, not wanting to slide into her and push her off the edge.

Penelope quickly spun around and stepped over Chiron's body. She held him firmly in place with her front legs as she inched her back legs toward the cliff edge.

"Clamp down on my tail," she screamed to Cloud.

Cloud grabbed a mouthful of hair and held on with all her strength. Penelope slowly started moving forward, being very careful to keep her footing on the loose, precarious slope.

Hank had hurriedly pulled Chiron to his feet and now the two of them grabbed Cloud's mane to help pull her the rest of the way up.

Meanwhile, on the trail above, Leonardo had Brutus in the ear pinch to beat all ear pinches. When Brutus had knocked Chiron down the slope, he himself was sent reeling right into Leonardo's path. Thinking quickly, Leonardo clamped his powerful jaws at the base of Brutus' ear and didn't let go. Brutus squealed in pain, but didn't move a muscle, in fear of losing his ear.

Leonardo knew that the kids could take care of themselves while he detained Brutus. They were an extremely capable bunch.

He was very relieved to see that Penelope had found the right path, at last. A family does so much better when every member helps and respects each other. The same is true of a herd.

Things were definitely looking up.

The group reconvened on the trail above and nuzzled each other in relief and joy until they realized that Leonardo was being very quiet. It was then they realized he had his mouth full and probably needed some assistance.

After relieving Leonardo of Brutus' ear, they needed to decide what to do with the scoundrel. After much debate, it was decided that Brutus should actually find the Minaret Peak unicorns and help them settle into their new home. Reports of his good works would be sent back periodically to Leonardo or there would be consequences that Brutus wouldn't like.

The rest of the weary group headed home. On the way, Leonardo talked to Cloud about becoming his apprentice. He would train her extensively in the healing arts while she lived in the Lolo Peak cave with him, his students, and, of course, Chiron. Cloud was honored and elated, but wanted to check with Plato first. They all knew Plato would give her his whole-hearted blessing.

Leonardo also had a great idea on the new leadership of Brutus', now leaderless, herd. Hank had proven himself a fine, upstanding unicorn and since he knew all there was to know about the herd, pending the herd's approval - Hank would be their new leader.

As for Penelope, her dream would finally come true. Leonardo suggested that while Cloud was living on Lolo Peak, Penelope help Plato in his work as herd healer. That, of course, would involve a lot of trips to Hank's valley to check on his herd's health. Penelope couldn't stop smiling, nor could Hank.

It looked like a happily ever after situation. Thank goodness everyone was too preoccupied with their happiness to see the ominous, black clouds slowly gathering overhead.

Book 3

The Dalian Migration

Chapter 1

Peace in the Valley

Peace had finally been restored to Paradise Valley. It had taken some near tragedies for everyone to realize how important their loved ones were, but now, love was abounding. Not only had Plato and Calypso been reunited at long last, but Cloud and Chiron were completely smitten with each other, and Penelope and Hank were headed in the same direction.

All was well with the world - or so it seemed.

Cloud had happily, and more than a little apprehensively, moved into Leonardo's cave near the jagged top of Lolo Peak. Her apprenticeship with the extraordinary healer was underway. This was an enormous honor. One she did not take lightly - thus the apprehension. Fully aware of the faith Leonardo had placed in her, she did not want to disappoint him.

Chiron was overjoyed at Cloud's success and proximity. There was a little more spring in his step as he ventured out early each morning to search for healthy and delicious plants. He did this not only to restock their stores but to keep Cloud pleasantly surprised by his amazing culinary skills. Leonardo wholeheartedly approved because he also got to partake in these scrumptious feasts.

Back in Paradise Valley, Penelope immediately took to her new role as her father's helper. She had a lot of forgiveness to earn after her hijinks and treachery in the previous weeks. She listened to and watched Plato carefully, absorbing every important piece of knowledge. She studied and cataloged all the plants she found during her walks in the surrounding forest. She kept a close eye on the bark strip baskets containing the many healing herbs in Plato's pharmacy, making sure they were full, should anyone need them.

She did this not only for Plato, but for Hank as well. She wanted to let him know his faith in her was much appreciated and even life-changing. Every time she made the trek to the neighboring valley to check on the health of his herd, she was on her absolute best behavior. Compassion was still hard for her to muster, but she gave it her best shot and was actually starting to realize its merits.

Weeks passed with everyone getting along and working well together. It looked like that dark chapter had ended for good. Until one stormy night . . .

That fateful day had started out as a beautiful morning. A dazzling, orange sunrise lit up a cloudless sky. It was the start of another perfect day. The unicorns went about their business - gathering food, frolicking in the wildflowers, and napping by the stream. All was well until just after the sun began its descent and the gathering clouds started to darken.

The herd was restless in the way only unicorns can get. They had an innate ability to sense danger, so they paced and whinnied and kept their loved ones close.

They had no way of knowing what was on the horizon. But they soon would be reminded of the mistakes of their forbearers.

Chapter 2

The Forbearers

Many decades earlier, during the great migration of the majestic animals of the Dalian Kingdom, a disagreement or two arose.

To maintain harmony within the kingdom, one representative from each of the great creatures sat on the Grand Council. The griffons elected Osiris as their spokesman, the youngest and most outspoken of their flock. His multi-colored feathers, imposing twelve foot wingspan, and long sharp talons, were enough to earn him the respect of the group. The unicorns had elected one of their wisest leaders, Hera, to speak for them. She was so white as to be almost translucent. Her startling purple eyes noticed everything. She could stand her own, with or without wings and talons. The dragons picked Zeus, the eldest dragon in their midst. They rightly assumed his 450 years of wisdom would prove useful.   He was astonishingly graceful, considering his enormous size. This grace and his glittering, metallic scales and massive, leathery wings gave him an air of dignity.

These noble creatures had lived peacefully side by side in Dalia for centuries, but a new, unfamiliar animal was creeping ever closer to their kingdom's boundaries. This strange, two-legged, wingless creature had dangerous weapons and a greed for land.

The Dalian scouts had been finding mammoths with puncture wounds in their sides. These sad discoveries were becoming more and more frequent and they were getting closer and closer to Dalia's secret, hidden realm. Fearing discovery and the same fate the mammoths met, it was decided by the inhabitants of Dalia that they would relocate to a more remote area. The Grand Council was thus convened.

Osiris and Zeus insisted their new home have steep mountains, dotted with plenty of deep caves for nesting. But Hera, being flightless, asked that they find a lush valley with plenty of green grass and a year-round stream. Dalia had all of these things. Finding a similar place would take time - something they did not have a lot of.

All three groups sent out scouts to search for this perfect place, only to have them return a few days later, exhausted and discouraged. In the meantime, a close watch was kept on the two-legged weapon throwers.

One stormy night, as lightning blazed and loud warnings thundered from the sky, a panicked watchman rushed back from his post. He hurriedly led the council representatives to the eastern edge of Dalia and pointed into the stormy blackness. A yellow glow quivered along the distant horizon. Just then, a lightning bolt lit up the sky, illuminating dozens of huge campfires in the distance. The throwers were close. Too close.

Chapter 3

The Great Migration Begins

Before the sun rose, messengers flew to each corner of Dalia to tell the inhabitants to collect their family members and anything they would need for a long journey. They were instructed to plan for the new life they would start at journey's end. They would be setting out into the unknown as soon as possible.

Young Leonardo, just a yearling, was already demonstrating the gift of foretelling. His friends knew to ask his advice whenever they needed to make an important decision. Leonardo was never wrong.

On this first day of the big migration, Leonardo was pacing and fretting.

"Please, we need to wait at least an hour," he pleaded with the council.

The stormy weather from the night before had caused the soil to loosen on the mountainsides. Leonardo had had a nightmarish vision of a huge mudslide roaring and crashing down a steep slope, catching the terrified unicorns unaware.

Knowing he was a skilled seer, the council agreed to wait exactly one hour, but only one hour. Leonardo bowed his head in agreement and hoped for the best.

When the anxious herd, weyr and flock could wait no longer, they set off from their gathering place on Dalia's western boundary. All of the griffon eggs had already hatched, but not so the dragon eggs. The dragons were able to carry most of the weyrs' eggs in their talons, but the rest of the leathery, speckled eggs had to be carried by the unicorns, along with a few baby griffons who were still too young to fly. This arrangement worked well. The baby griffons climbed upon the unicorns' backs, their talons gripped the long, fine hair of the unicorns' manes while their tightly-folded wings securely held the dragon eggs. Unicorns are extremely sure-footed and griffons have very powerful talons and wings, so this was an ingenious solution.

The massive assemblage got underway heading toward the mountain pass that would lead them to the high plains and then further into the great unknown.

It was early afternoon when word arrived from the lead dragons that a massive slide of rocks, mud and broken trees had obliterated the trail through the mountains. The dragons heard the roaring mud and rock just before they flew over it and witnessed its devastation first hand. It happened exactly an hour before the unicorns arrived.

Everyone turned toward Leonardo. He humbly shrugged, nearly knocking the young griffon passenger off his back.

"We're all okay. That's what counts," he said matter-of-factly. "Now let's figure out how to get around it."

There was only one way to get everyone over the deep, sticky mud, huge boulders and gigantic downed trees. The dragons and griffons would have to carry each unicorn over the slide until all were safely on the other side. They set to work crafting carriers from tree branches. The sturdy branches would go under the unicorn's stomach and the strongest of the dragons and griffons would each grasp one end of the carrier in their talons and carefully fly their heavy cargo across the slide. The unicorns, though apprehensive, decided it was better than walking the many steep, dangerous miles around the slide or staying put to face the throwers.

It was a long and arduous process, with a close call or two when the branches would snap midway over the massive slide. Those unlucky unicorns were hurriedly grabbed and carried by their manes and tails, but prefered that to being dropped into the deep mud below.

When all the unicorns, eggs, and hatchlings were safely across the mudslide, the group continued into the unknown. The first unicorns across the mud had set out ahead in hopes of finding a suitable area to bed down for the night. The rest of the group soon caught up, exhausted and shaken.

A lush meadow surrounded by huge pines at the base of the mountain was the chosen spot. The progress they had hoped for was not to be, but they stayed optimistic regardless. They huddled together and soon fell into the deep sleep of the truly weary. All, that is, but the council.

Tania Liu

At first light the huge group set out again. A debate about which direction to take had kept the leaders up late into the night, but after a very heated discussion, a consensus was finally reached. They would head north toward some high, jagged peaks the scouts had discovered on one of their missions. Hera had argued against it, wanting to go southwest toward the low lying hills and grassy plains, but had been overruled by Zeus and Osiris. The unicorns were a tough lot, reasoned Hera. They would adapt to the mountains.

The huge assemblage steadfastly ambled onward. They passed through pine- filled valleys and crossed wide rivers. They stopped when exhausted to rest and, hopefully, find enough food to keep their strength up. At night, they would gather close and the elders would weave grandiose tales of their many youthful adventures. But none came close to the one they were all on now.

The massive peaks of their new home revealed themselves on the fourth day. They were beautiful, rugged and, best of all, remote.

The mood of the group was lifted by this far off glimpse of their new home. It was still many miles away, but at least the end was in sight. Elaborate stories of warm caves and lush grasses circulated through the optimistic group as they trudged onward. Everyone was excited and joyful, except Leonardo.

He had been experiencing a recurring vision. A dark, foreboding vision. It wasn't clear enough for him to make any sense of it. He had blurry glimpses of raging water and sharp talons. All he knew for certain was that it filled him with dread.

Chapter 4

The Last River Crossing - Part I

Leonardo awoke with a start. Huge raindrops were splashing on and around him. He carefully straightened his front legs, so as not to wake up the young griffon curled up against him.

He had become quite fond of his young griffon passenger, Odin. During this long trek to their new homeland, they had plenty of time to get to know each other. Odin was smart, curious and fearless. Traits he shared with Leonardo.

Leonardo slowly and carefully got to his feet to assess this unfriendly weather situation. As he studied the dark, roiling clouds, he made sure Odin was staying warm and dry beneath him.

Craig Key

A loud thunder crack woke Odin with a start. The rest of the assemblage was likewise startled by this rude awakening. As the shivering, wet animals gathered together to hear the day's plan, they were surprised to find the council members pacing and whispering back and forth, apparently disagreeing on what to tell the group.

"Dalians, I have some bad news," shouted Zeus. "Our scouts tell us that we have only one more river crossing before we get to our destination. Unfortunately, the storm has caused the water level of this river to rise dangerously."

"Oh, come on. How bad could it be?" yelled Jupiter, Zeus' son.

Jupiter was nothing like his father. Where Zeus was wise and cautious, Jupiter was foolish and brash.

"The river is treacherous enough for us to wait another two days for the waters to recede," stated Hera. "I will not risk one unicorn life just to get to the mountains sooner. If the weather clears up before the waters recede, we can attempt to lift the unicorns with branches as we did over the mudslide, but in this pouring rain, that would be far too dangerous to attempt."

"The dragons and griffons will stay with the unicorns to help protect them should the throwers catch up. We stick together," stated Zeus matter-of-factly.

"That's not fair!" bellowed Jupiter. "The unicorns have gotten this far by crossing many rivers. I'm not waiting with them for two whole days while the throwers get closer. Maybe the poor unicorns are weak and frightened, but that's not my problem. Who's strong enough to come with me?"

"Zeus and Hera are right," yelled Leonardo. "I've had a terrifying vision of dangerous, raging water."

"You and your visions. I'm sick of hearing that mumbo jumbo!" shouted Jupiter. "You can't control the whole group with your make-believe. You're just trying to earn some status with the dragons by going along with whatever Zeus says. Well, not today. You're leading the unicorns across the river with Odin on your back, carrying my egg. Yes, my one and only egg. That is how strongly I feel about the importance and safety of this crossing. You who are too fearful to come along can wait for the throwers to show up and have you for dinner."

There were shocked gasps and rumblings through the group.

"If Jupiter is willing to risk his only egg, it must be safe," shouted one unicorn. Others agreed and soon a small contingent of unicorns stood next to Jupiter.

Leonardo tried to reason with them. He brought up his mudslide prediction, but memories are short, and the fear of the throwers was too strong. Soon he was being pushed to the front of the group.

Another group of unicorns stood off to the side, arguing loudly. After several minutes, one approached Leonardo.

"You will prove your bravery and the bravery of all the unicorns by leading us safely across the river," stated the spokesman for the unicorns. "We have discussed the pros and cons, and we've decided we can't risk everyone's life by our unwillingness to take this chance. Jupiter is right - we've crossed many rivers safely. We can't jeopardize this mission when it is so close to being completed."

With that, the assembled unicorns spoke up, giving words of encouragement and advice to Leonardo.

"Just take it slowly," "Don't worry," "You can do it," "We have faith in you".

"Enough chit-chat! Time is of the essence," yelled Jupiter as he signaled for his wife, Venus, to bring their egg to him. She hesitated for a moment, then moved slowly toward Jupiter. She knew that if things went awry, she could always fly out and grab her egg. A dangerous maneuver in the pouring rain, but one she would be more than willing to do to save her egg.

Leonardo walked slowly toward the steep, muddy riverbank. As he stood there studying the crashing, roiling water of the river, Odin appeared at his side.

"We can do this," Odin said softly. "But we better hurry. My parents are freaking out. I told them I was going to tell you I couldn't do it, but I know if I don't, Jupiter will just find a replacement for me, and besides, I can't abandon you."

Odin then shook out his soaked feathers and flew awkwardly toward Leonardo's slippery back, finally landing it on his third attempt. It didn't inspire confidence.

Jupiter seemed unfazed by the horrible weather, the raging river, or by Odin's clumsy attempts at getting on Leonardo's back. He marched over to Odin and handed him his precious egg.

"Now go," he ordered. "We will be flying overhead and will meet you on the other side."

It was decided that Leonardo and Odin would cross with two bareback unicorns following closely, should anything go amiss. Any other unicorns carrying young griffons and eggs would wait on the bank until the crossing was proven to be safe. Most griffon and dragon parents elected to carry their young and eggs themselves, choosing to make multiple trips back and forth, knowing full well the risk of dropping their very slippery cargos, but deciding it was the safer choice. They realized that Jupiter was just trying to prove his point - as reckless as it seemed.

Leonardo took a deep breath, told Odin to hang on tightly, and bravely started down the steep bank. He could hear Odin's panicked parents yelling at him to stop, but it was too late.

Things went terribly wrong with his first step. Just as he started down the bank, it gave way underneath his hooves and he started sliding toward the raging water, completely out of control.

The rampaging water had dug away at the muddy bank, leaving a deep eddy of swirling water at the bottom. Leonardo tried to dig his hooves into the mud hoping to slow their descent, but to no avail. If anything, they were gaining speed as the deep, forbidding whirlpool waited impatiently to swallow them up.

Just then Leonardo had an idea. It was a crazy one, but he didn't have a lot of options at this point. Instead of trying to stop, he decided to speed up and when the time was right he would launch them over the rapidly-spinning eddy and, hopefully, land in the calmer water on the far side.

He leaned downhill and relaxed his legs just enough to start gliding along the top of the mud. It was working. They were flying toward the water, but was it too little, too late? He couldn't worry about that now. As he neared the water, he bent his legs as far down as they would go and straightened up with a sudden springing motion.

They were literally flying now. As the crowd on the banks stood aghast, Leonardo, Odin and the speckled egg went airborne, flying over the dangerous whirlpool. It seemed to take forever for them to finally land in the calmer water on the far side of the eddy.

A huge sigh of relief went through the crowd, but was followed by another bout of terror, as Leonardo and his passengers landed with a splash and immediately sank under the deep water.

No one moved as they anxiously watched the river for signs of the brave souls. Just when it seemed hopeless, up bobbed Leonardo's head, then Odin appeared, clinging on fiercely to Leonardo's soggy mane, the egg clutched securely in his wings. As the water ran down their heads and into their eyes, the raging current tossed them about. They were totally disoriented and seemed to be flailing helplessly when suddenly they reached a calm spot in the river. The momentary lull was just enough for Leonardo to get his bearings and start forcefully paddling toward the far bank.

The crowd cheered, as the next two unicorns hurriedly jumped down the bank and, following Leonardo's lead, launched over the whirlpool. They wanted to catch up to Leonardo should he need any help.

They needn't have rushed. They couldn't have caught up to Leonardo if they wanted to. The wild, treacherous river was totally in control. They were being tossed around like rag dolls. All they could do was aim in the right direction and paddle with all they had.

Leonardo seemed to be holding his own. He was already halfway across and looking strong. That was, until the log showed up.

Chapter 5

The Last River Crossing - Part II

"We've got this," shouted Leonardo, as he plotted a course toward a suitable landing place on the far bank.

Odin let out a big sigh of relief. Suddenly something caught his eye and he turned his head upriver.

"LOOK OUT," he screamed, as the huge log bore down on them like a battering ram.

"DUCK," yelled Leonardo, but it was too late. There was no way out of this one.

Both Odin and Leonardo closed their eyes, waiting for the inevitable collision.

Seconds passed and nothing happened. When the weary crossers opened their eyes, the log was gone. Looking up, Odin couldn't believe what he was seeing. Osiris had the massive log clasped firmly in his huge talons, his wings beating furiously. Water poured off the immense log as it swayed and lurched precariously through the air. It was a tough struggle, but he managed to hang onto it just long enough to drop it downriver. He had saved their lives.

It looked like they were in the clear. The opposite shore was in sight and the river seemed to be getting calmer. But looks can be deceiving.

Leonardo had never heard of an undertow - a powerful current that secretly awaits unsuspecting swimmers by hiding its rapidly moving water just below the surface.

When Leonardo's legs were suddenly pushed sideways out from under him, he learned firsthand what an undertow was. He quickly found himself under the churning water. He wasn't sure which way was up. His nostrils were stinging from the water he had breathed in.

As he flailed helplessly against the current, he realized that Odin was no longer grasping his mane. Panic set in. Odin was too little to deal with the raging river on his own. And what of Venus and Jupiter's egg?

With renewed vigor, Leonardo fought until his head broke through to the surface. He realized he was far downstream from the original crossing point. He couldn't worry about that now. He had to find Odin. But, as much as he desperately searched the surrounding water, there was no sign of him. Undeterred, he kept spinning in circles, frantically looking in every direction. Nothing.

Just as despair started setting in, Leonardo heard a faint sound. He spun toward it, but saw nothing but white caps. As a wave lifted him above the surface, he caught sight of Odin downstream, struggling to stay afloat against the raging current, bravery mixed with terror filled his eyes. Leonardo tried desperately to swim toward him, but was helpless against the powerful current. Odin was sinking and fighting to resurface, over and over. Leonardo could see he was exhausted by the fight. Just when Odin sank for what looked like it would be the last time. Leonardo, adrenaline pumping, pushed off from a submerged boulder and rocketed through the turbulent water to Odin's location. He took a deep breath and lunged under the water. Odin was flailing helplessly, toppling head over heels through the current. Leonardo grabbed him with his teeth and swam for the surface. As they burst out of the water, Leonardo lost his grip on Odin. Panic stricken and near exhaustion, he tried to lunge for his fast-moving friend. A gust from gigantic wings rippled the water's surface and Odin was suddenly airborne. Leonardo looked up in shock to see Odin safely clasped in his father's talons. Osiris had saved his life once again.

Finally, Leonardo was able to swim to the far shore. He collapsed, completely exhausted, on the bank. He noticed Venus and some other dragons flying overhead, but was too tired to move his head to see what they were doing. It was later that he learned that Venus and Jupiter's egg had been washed downstream and was never found. Don't despair, things have a way of working out in the long run.

Chapter 6

The Parting of Ways

After the horrible disaster that befell Leonardo and Odin, the rest of the dragons and griffons waited for the rainstorm to let up and then carried their own young and eggs over the unforgiving river.

Jupiter somehow convinced his fellow dragons that the tragic happenings of that fateful day were all Leonardo's fault. He told them Leonardo had brought it on himself with his mystical visions. By disrespecting Mother Nature with his predictions of her ill will, she had made him pay for his insolence. The dragons may have gone along with him in sympathy for his loss or because his father was their leader - we'll never know for sure. But, Osiris and the rest of the griffons were unconvinced by this theory.

An insurmountable rift soon formed between the three groups. Tensions rose to a fever pitch and it became readily apparent that the era of their peaceful coexistence was at an end.

The dragons laid claim to the jagged peaks they were approaching, while the griffons and unicorns decided to go elsewhere. Since they each wanted different things, the unicorns decided to search for a fertile valley, while the griffons would look for a suitable mountain range.

The groups said their goodbyes and went their separate ways. The griffons were out of sight over the horizon in no time, while the unicorns plodded slowly on, heads down, wearily searching for their perfect home.

Leonardo was so distraught by these developments, he decided to exile himself on the steepest, loneliest mountain he could find. He would live alone in a cave and dedicate the rest of his life to helping those who needed it.

His mother, Hera, tried to convince him to reconsider, but when he wouldn't, she told him she would support his decision. All she could do was hope he would change his mind one day. After saying their tearful goodbyes, Hera lead her distraught herd to a beautiful valley not far from the peak Leonardo chose. They dubbed it Paradise Valley. Years later, Hera had a new colt. She named him Plato.

Many decades passed. Leonardo had still not changed his mind. He still lived on his steep, jagged mountain, Lolo Peak. He made good on his intention of helping others and was revered, far and wide, for his knowledge and compassion.

That brings us back to Paradise Valley and the calamity that was on the horizon.

Chapter 7

Just Another Perfect Day

Just before midnight, it happened. A low rumble started from the core of the Earth. The ground started shaking violently. Trees toppled and cracks formed in the meadow, separating large areas of grass and wildflowers into long, thin islands.

Panicked unicorns ran in all directions, not knowing which way was safe. Plato tried to keep everyone calm, but the noise and chaos drowned out his shouts of reassurance.

Penelope considered abandoning the herd and running as fast and as far as she could go, but her newfound concern for others, young and old, overtook her. She ran onto the speaking mound and reared as high as she could go, flailing her hooves in the air as she bellowed at the top of her lungs. The noise and commotion caught the herd's attention and they all gathered around.

As soon as the herd's pacing and snorting was at a minimum, Penelope began to speak.

"Listen up! We need to take some deep breaths and calm down. The one place not affected by the shaking is the creek bed. Gather your loved ones and carefully make your way into the creek," she said with authority.

The unicorns all turned to look toward the creek and could immediately see she was right. The creek was unchanged. The inevitable stampede toward the creek began when the ground started shaking harder.

The entire herd was safely standing in the creek when the terrifying rumbling finally stopped. Penelope and Plato walked up and down the creek, checking the herd for any injuries, when Penelope noticed movement in the distance. She could just make out Hank and the rest of his herd on the edge of the valley, carefully making their way toward the creek to help and console Plato's herd.

While Penelope was bravely protecting her herd, Cloud was doing much the same atop Lolo Peak.

All of Leonardo's students had been sound asleep in his cave when the rumbling began. It started as a low growl that soon escalated into a roar as it echoed throughout the cave's many chambers.

Cloud, being a light sleeper, was the first one to hear it. She ran from chamber to chamber alerting everyone of the potential danger. Though she'd never experienced anything like this before, she'd heard tales of such devastation. It didn't take her long to realize the cave could collapse.

Unfortunately, the narrow trail outside the cave was no safer, the huge boulders bouncing toward it from above were enough to send the panicked group back toward the cave, right after Cloud had managed to get them all out.

Cloud, Chiron and Leonardo were finishing their final cave inspection, making sure everyone was safely out, when they heard the terrified whinnies coming from the entrance.

BLM.gov

Boulders were falling like huge hailstones breaking off edges of the already narrow trail. The panicked unicorns darted back and forth, slipping precariously on the rocky trail.

Leonardo pushed his way out of the cave and onto the trail, yelling at the top of lungs, "Follow me!"

He reared up and spun on his heels. It seemed he was about to fall off the edge of the mountain. Instead, he led the way to the trail's dead end. Leonardo then turned toward the mountain and pushed a huge bush aside to reveal a long, dark tunnel through the rock. On the far side of the tunnel was a steep trail that zig-zagged down through the forest.

It would have been a perfect answer to their predicament, except a huge rock slab dislodged from the roof of the tunnel just then, shattering onto the ground below, taking most of the roof with it. Their escape tunnel was completely blocked.

Panic ensued. The unicorns were pushing and shoving, trying desperately to avoid the rocks crashing down around them. Just then, a terrified, young stallion swung around on the trail, bashing into Leonardo. Unable to maintain his footing on the loose rock, Leonardo plunged over the edge of the steep cliff.

"NO!" screamed Cloud in horror, as she fought her way to the edge.

Just then a rush of air blew her mane into her face. She shook her hair back just in time to see the tip of an enormous, multi-colored wing pass before her eyes.

The huge griffon folded its wings back, forming a wedge shape, as it dove toward Leonardo. Its massive talons reached out and encircled the falling unicorn, lifting him into the air just a few feet before he would have hit the ground. At the same moment, the gigantic wings opened like a parachute and stopped them both in mid-air. It was a miraculous sight.

Leonardo was shaken up, but managed a weak smile, as he looked up at his rescuer.

"Thanks, Odin," he said.

Chapter 8

The Much-Overdo Reconciliation

The sky above Lolo Peak was suddenly teeming with griffons. And just as suddenly a group of dragons flew overhead. They all swooped down, snatching the falling rocks in mid-air and dropping them far from the startled, but very grateful, unicorns.

As soon as the rumbling stopped, the griffons and dragons began clearing the trail of fallen rock. The unicorns joined in and soon the path was open. The exhausted group slowly and carefully made their way down to Paradise Valley.

When they rounded the last turn in the trail, no one could believe their eyes. Paradise Valley, or what was left of it, lay before them in ruin. The ground was torn apart - deep crevasses criss-crossed the meadow, fallen trees lay every which way. It was a disaster of epic proportions.

Penelope, with Hank at her side, led her group of shaken-up unicorns out of the creek bed, while Cloud, with Chiron at her side, led her group of equally shaken-up unicorns from the Lolo Peak trail. They met somewhere near the middle of the valley, with tears streaming down their faces.

"What do we do now?" they muttered in unison.

Leonardo, Plato and Hera stood in the devastated meadow, their necks intertwined. With tears filling their eyes they didn't need to say a word. They were so grateful that no one had been hurt.

Venus stood nearby with a shockingly beautiful dragon at her side. He had shimmering silver scales and enormous golden talons. Everyone grew quiet and stared at the striking pair.

Venus began to speak, "Unicorns of Paradise Valley, when we heard tell of your calamity, we immediately flew from our home in the Bitterroot Mountains to assist you in any way we could. I am the new leader of the dragons. Zeus and Jupiter have temporarily left the weyr to find harmony.

This is my son, Mercury. The older of you might remember him as the speckled egg that washed down the river. As it turned out, a group of swans found his egg washed up on shore. They carefully rolled it into their nest where they watched over it until it hatched. They lovingly raised Mercury until he was old enough to fly. He knew he had a dragon family somewhere and has spent years searching for us. As luck would have it, he was searching in this area today just as his weyr flew over Lolo Peak. We recognized each other instantly. Thank goodness he wouldn't give up. He finally found us. It appears he has found us all."

A cheer rose from the crowd.

Odin and Leonardo made their way to the center of the group to stand with Venus and Mercury.

"This has been an awful, yet wonderful, day. Do not despair for Paradise Valley", shouted Leonardo. "Instead, I would like you all to meet my good friend, Odin. He just told me something heartwarming. Apparently, he, along with his fellow griffons, has been watching over the unicorns for decades. Many years ago we were very close, but a tragedy separated us. A tragedy involving an egg that was lost in a raging river. Well, that separation is now over."

Odin nodded his head and began to speak, "We are here to offer our services in your time of need. We live on Mount Sentinel, a magnificent mountain on the far side of Crystal Peak. Between our home and Crystal Peak lies a lush valley. We would be honored to have you live there as our guests while Paradise Valley recovers from this awful event. We will help Mother Nature along by carrying away the fallen trees and bringing in dirt and rock to fill in these cracks. We will have you back in your beautiful home as soon as possible, but we plan on being a part of your lives from this moment on. This separation has been hard on all of us and we feel the time has come to rekindle lost friendships."

Venus, Mercury, Hera and Leonardo couldn't stop smiling and enthusiastically nodded in agreement as they watched the herds, weyr and flock begin happily mingling.

The majestic creatures of Dalia would be one again.

Thank you for accompanying Cloud and Penelope on their many adventures.

I hope you enjoyed yourself.

For more information on this and other books by Jill A. Logan, please visit her Facebook page or email her at "soapsuds785@aol.com".